HISTORICAL PERSPECTIVES
In Their Own Words

The Words of LEWIS AND CLARK

I0801611

Emmett Martin

PowerKiDS press

Published in 2024 by The Rosen Publishing Group, Inc.
2544 Clinton Street, Buffalo, NY 14224

Copyright © 2024 by The Rosen Publishing Group, Inc.

All rights reserved. No part of this book may be reproduced in any form without permission in writing from the publisher, except by a reviewer.

Portions of this work were originally authored by Janey Levy and published as *Lewis and Clark in Their Own Words.* All new material in this edition was authored by Emmett Martin.

Editor: Therese Shea
Book Design: Michael Flynn

Photo Credits: Cover (Lewis and Clark) Everett Collection/Shutterstock.com; (series background) merrymuuu/Shutterstock.com; (fact box) Miloje/Shutterstock.com; p. 5 (map) courtesy of the Library of Congress; p. 5 (Jefferson's letter) Records of the United States House of Representatives, Record Group 233, National Archives; p. 7 https://commons.wikimedia.org/wiki/File:Clark_Family_Collection-_Volume_1._Voorhis_Journal_No._1,_April_7-July_3,_1805._Back_cover.jpg; p. 8 https://commons.wikimedia.org/wiki/File:Missouri_indian_Oto_indian_and_chief_of_the_Puncas_0040v.jpg; p. 9 https://en.m.wikipedia.org/wiki/File:Charles_Floyd.jpg; p. 11 https://commons.wikimedia.org/wiki/File:SIOUX_CHIEF.JPG; p. 13 https://commons.wikimedia.org/wiki/File:Fort_Mandan.JPG; p. 15 (grizzly bear) Scott E. Read/Shutterstock.com; p. 15 (bison) Nicholas J. Klein/Shutterstock.com; p. 17 Joseph Sohm/Shutterstock.com; p. 19 https://commons.wikimedia.org/wiki/File:Lewis_and_Clark_Reach_Shoshone_Camp_Led_by_Sacajawea.jpg; p. 21 (Bitterroot Mountains) Nicholas Courtney/Shutterstock.com; p. 21 (inset) https://commons.wikimedia.org/wiki/File:George_Catlin_-_H%27co-a-h%27co-a-h%27cotes-min,_No_Horns_on_His_Head,_a_Brave_-_1985.66.146_-_Smithsonian_American_Art_Museum.jpg; p. 23 Paul Street/Alamy Stock Photo; p. 25 https://commons.wikimedia.org/wiki/File:Lewis_and_clark-expedition.jpg; p. 27 steve estvanik/Shutterstock.com; p. 29 https://commons.wikimedia.org/wiki/File:Lewis_and_Clark_Expedition_map.svg.

Library of Congress Cataloging-in-Publication Data

Names: Martin, Emmett, author.
Title: The words of Lewis and Clark / Emmett Martin.
Description: New York : PowerKids Press, [2024] | Series: Historical perspectives : in their own words | Includes bibliographical references and index.
Identifiers: LCCN 2022052190 (print) | LCCN 2022052191 (ebook) | ISBN 9781642827040 (library binding) | ISBN 9781642827033 (paperback) | ISBN 9781642827057 (ebook)
Subjects: LCSH: Lewis and Clark Expedition (1804-1806)--Juvenile literature. | Lewis, Meriwether, 1774-1809--Diaries--Juvenile literature. | Clark, William, 1770-1838--Diaries--Juvenile literature. | Explorers--West (U.S.)--Diaries--Juvenile literature. | West (U.S.)--Discovery and exploration--Juvenile literature.
Classification: LCC F592.7 .M28 2024 (print) | LCC F592.7 (ebook) | DDC 917.804/2--dc23/eng/20221028
LC record available at https://lccn.loc.gov/2022052190
LC ebook record available at https://lccn.loc.gov/2022052191

Manufactured in the United States of America

Some of the images in this book illustrate individuals who are models. The depictions do not imply actual situations or events.

CPSIA Compliance Information: Batch #CSPK24. For further information contact Rosen Publishing at 1-800-237-9932.

Find us on

CONTENTS

THE LOUISIANA TERRITORY

At the beginning of 1803, the United States was much smaller than it is today. It stretched from the Atlantic Ocean in the east to the Mississippi River in the west. France owned territory to the west of the Mississippi. At first, U.S. president Thomas Jefferson tried to buy New Orleans, a port at the mouth of the Mississippi, from France. But then France offered its entire Louisiana Territory, including New Orleans. The United States agreed. This land would nearly double the size of the nation.

Maps of that time showed large empty spaces within the Louisiana Territory because mapmakers knew little about the region. President Jefferson charged his secretary, Meriwether Lewis, with leading an expedition to explore the land. Lewis asked his friend William Clark to lead the expedition with him.

LOOKING BACK

French leader Napoleon Bonaparte authorized the sale of the Louisiana Territory to help pay for wars that France was fighting at that time. In 1804, he declared himself French emperor.

Secret Mission

In January 1803, before the Louisiana Territory was purchased, Jefferson asked Congress in secret to fund an expedition west. He explained the expedition would improve knowledge about Native Americans of the region and promote trade with them. The expedition would also explore the Missouri River and attempt to find a water route to the Pacific Ocean, a route some called the Northwest Passage. Five months later, on May 2, the United States purchased the Louisiana Territory.

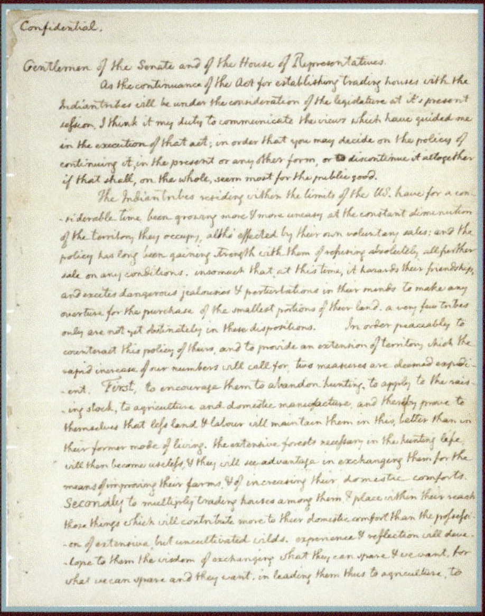

Confidential.

Gentlemen of the Senate and of the House of Representatives.

As the continuance of the Act for establishing trading houses with the Indian tribes will be under the consideration of the legislature at it's present session, I think it my duty to communicate the views which have guided me in the execution of that act; in order that you may decide on the policy of continuing it, in the present or any other form, or discontinue it altogether if that shall, on the whole, seem most for the public good.

The Indian tribes residing within the limits of the U.S. have for a considerable time been growing more & more uneasy at the constant diminution of the territory they occupy, altho' effected by their own voluntary sales: and the policy has long been gaining strength with them of refusing absolutely all further sale on any conditions. insomuch that, at this time, it hazards their friendship, and excites dangerous jealousies & perturbations in their minds to make any overture for the purchase of the smallest portions of their land. a very few tribes only are not yet obstinately in these dispositions. In order peaceably to counteract this policy of theirs, and to provide an extension of territory which the rapid increase of our numbers will call for, two measures are deemed expedient. First, to encourage them to abandon hunting, to apply to the raising stock, to agriculture and domestic manufacture, and thereby prove to themselves that less land & labour will maintain them in this, better than in their former mode of living. the extensive forests necessary in the hunting life, will then become useless, & they will see advantage in exchanging them for the means of improving their farms, & of increasing their domestic comforts. Secondly to multiply trading houses among them, & place within their reach those things which will contribute more to their domestic comfort than the possession of extensive, but uncultivated wilds. experience & reflection will develope to them the wisdom of exchanging what they can spare & we want, for what we can spare and they want. in leading them thus to agriculture, to

Jefferson's request to Congress, January 1803

The Louisiana Territory stretched from the Mississippi River to the Rocky Mountains and from the Gulf of Mexico to Canada.

PACKING FOR THE JOURNEY

Getting ready for an expedition across the largely unmapped Louisiana Territory was a challenging task in itself. To prepare, Lewis and Clark studied mapmaking, plant life, medicine, and other areas of science that might be helpful on their journey. They also had to assemble a team, have a special boat built, and buy supplies and equipment. Equipment included a compass, thermometers, kettles, spoons, rope, a mill for grinding corn, and gifts for Native American peoples, including scissors.

People studying about the expedition today learn a lot from the journals of Lewis and Clark. At least five other members of the expedition kept journals as well. The spelling and **punctuation** in these journals may look strange to us today. For example, Lewis spelled the word scissors "*scizors*."

LOOKING BACK

The Louisiana Territory was named for French king Louis XIV in 1682.

York

An enslaved man named York was the only African American expedition member. He was enslaved from birth by William Clark's family. Clark and York had grown up together. York was an equal member of the expedition, taking part in all activities. When Clark and three others were caught in a storm, York risked his life to search for them. York expected to be freed after the expedition. Clark refused, at least at first. York's final fate is unknown.

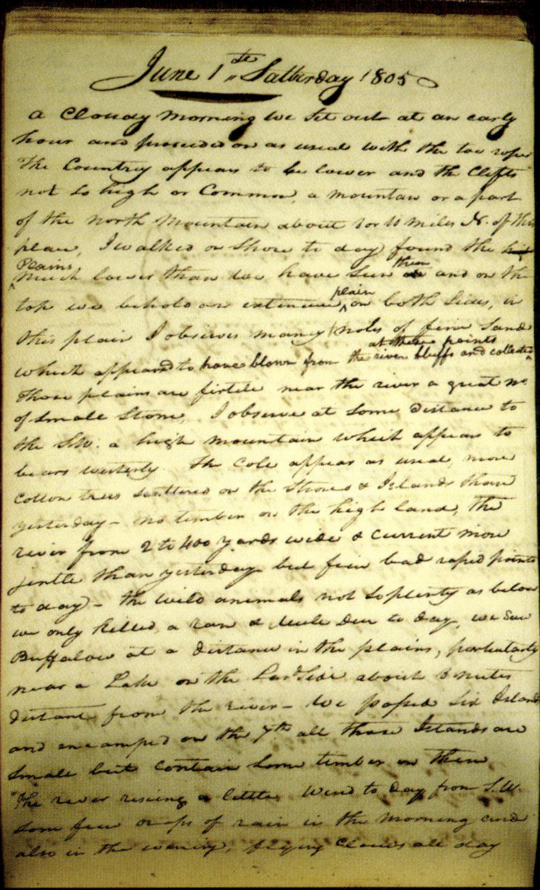

William Clark's journal

During the time of Lewis and Clark, people used different spellings for the same word. Some misspellings and odd punctuation and capitalization in the expedition's journals are because the writers didn't have a lot of education.

SETTING OUT

On May 14, 1804, the expedition west began. The group, sometimes called the **Corps** of Discovery, started out from St. Louis, Missouri. In his journal, Clark recorded the gloomy weather that day: "I Set out at 4 oClock P.M. . . . and proceeded on under a jentle brease [gentle breeze] up the Missourie [Missouri River] . . . a heavy rain this after-noon."

On August 3, 1804, the Corps of Discovery had its first official encounter with Native Americans. The explorers exchanged gifts with the Otoe and Missouria tribes. Clark wrote, "Sent them Some rosted [roasted] meat, Pork flour & meal, in return they sent us Water millions [watermelons]."

Meriwether Lewis promised the United States would trade with the Otoe and Missouria as long as they kept peace with the Omaha people.

Miscommunication

Cultural and language differences meant it wasn't always easy for the Corps of Discovery to talk with the Native American peoples they met. For example, in the first meeting with the Otoe people, they gave a medal to a man who wasn't the head of the tribe. This caused problems within the tribe. However, a second meeting was more successful. In March 1805, a group of these Native Americans traveled to Washington, D.C., to meet with President Jefferson.

LOOKING BACK

Around the time of this first meeting with Native Americans, two members of the expedition deserted the group. One later escaped for good, while another was brought back and punished.

Most of the members of the Corps of Discovery were volunteers from the U.S. Army, including Charles Floyd. Floyd was the only member of the expedition to die, after he became ill during the summer of 1804.

Near the end of August 1804, the Corps of Discovery encountered Yankton Sioux people in South Dakota. They held a council with them at Calumet Bluff, a hill in today's Cedar County, Nebraska. Their bison-skin **tepees** and orderly villages impressed Clark, who wrote, "The Scioues [Sioux's] Camps are handsom [handsome] of a Conic form Covered with Buffalow Roabs [robes] . . . and all compact & handsomly arranged."

Clark noted the people's strength and was particularly struck by the warriors, with their war paint, porcupine **quills**, and feathers. He recorded their appearance in some detail: "The Warriers [warriors] are Verry much deckerated [decorated] with Paint Porcupine quils & feathers, large leagins [leggings] and mockersons [moccasins], all with buffalow roabs [robes] of Different Colours."

LOOKING BACK

The American bison was often called buffalo in the United States and Canada. However, true buffalo don't live naturally in North America.

The Missing Omaha

It is uncertain if the Corps of Discovery met with Omaha people. As they passed by two Omaha villages in August 1804, they discovered they were abandoned. Like many other Native Peoples, the Omaha had been nearly wiped out by smallpox, a terrible disease brought to North America by European colonists. Clark recorded: "I am told when this fatal **malady** was among them they Carried their franzey [**frenzy**] to verry extroardinary [extraordinary] length . . . burning their Village."

This Oglala Sioux Elder holds a medal given to Native American leaders by the Corps of Discovery.

FORT MANDAN WINTER

In late October 1804, the Corps of Discovery arrived at the villages of the Mandan and Hidatsa peoples, near present-day Bismarck, North Dakota. They needed warm shelter for the winter, so Lewis and Clark chose a nearby spot to build a fort. Fort Mandan was completed by December.

During the winter, Lewis and Clark continued preparations for the rest of the journey. To help them communicate with Native Americans farther west, they hired Toussaint Charbonneau, a French-Canadian trapper, as an interpreter. He had a young Shoshone wife named Sacagawea.

By mid-February 1805, the expedition had run out of meat. They hunted when possible, but as Lewis complained, the wolves often ate what the hunters killed. Finally, in early April, the expedition set out again.

LOOKING BACK

The Corps named the fort "in honour of our Neighbours," the Mandan people. The Mandan and Hidatsa villages were home to about 4,500 Native Americans at that time.

Dangerously Cold

The winter of 1804–1805 was an extremely cold one. Clark made entries recording the temperature. On December 8, 1804, he wrote, "The Thermometer Stood at 12 d [degrees] below 0 which is 42 d below the freesing [freezing] point." Soon, it was colder. It was 21 degrees Fahrenheit below zero (-29°C) on December 11 and 38 degrees Fahrenheit below zero (-39°C) on December 12. On December 17, Clark recorded: "45 d. below 0." Some expedition members, including York, suffered from **frostbite**.

Fort Mandan has been reconstructed. It would have looked like this. The pickets were protection against hostile Native Americans.

HEADING WEST AGAIN

On April 7, 1805, the expedition was ready to travel again. Lewis and Clark sent the largest boat and about 12 men back down the Missouri River, along with maps, reports, Native American objects, and scientific specimens for President Jefferson. The permanent party—Lewis, Clark, York, Charbonneau, Sacagawea, Sacagawea's baby boy, and 27 soldiers—headed west. Lewis recorded his excitement and that of the whole party: "I could but esteem this moment of my departure as among the most happy of my life. The party are in excellent health and sperits [spirits] . . . and anxious to proceed."

As they journeyed west, the explorers were astonished by the plentiful wildlife, including elks, antelopes, and bison herds numbering 10,000. They also remarked how tame the animals seemed.

LOOKING BACK

The specimens sent to Jefferson contained corn, animal skins and skeletons, mineral samples, and five live animals, including a prairie dog.

Grizzly Bear!

The expedition provided the first scientific description of the grizzly bear, calling it "grisley." Native Americans had told the explorers about the bears, but the expedition didn't encounter one until late April 1805. Lewis recorded his experience: "It is a much more furious and formidable anamal [animal], and will frequently pursue the hunter when wounded. it is astonishing to see the wounds they will bear before they can be put to death. the Indians may well fear this anamal."

Around 50 million bison lived on the plains of North America when Europeans arrived. Overhunting nearly brought them to extinction.

OBSTACLES BEFORE THE ROCKIES

On May 26, 1805, Meriwether Lewis saw the Rocky Mountains ahead. He wrote, "When I reflected on the difficulties which this snowey [snowy] barrier would most probably throw in my way to the Pacific, and the sufferings and hardships of myself and party in thim [them], it in some measure counterballanced [counterbalanced] the joy I had felt."

A few days later, June 2, the expedition reached a fork in the Missouri River and had to choose a way. Lewis scouted ahead on the south, looking for the Great Falls the Hidatsa had told them about. He found it—it was actually five waterfalls. They chose the south branch of the river, the correct route, but the expedition had to carry everything more than 18 miles (29 km) to get around the falls.

LOOKING BACK

It took the Corps of Discovery about a month to portage around the Great Falls. To portage means to carry a boat between waters.

Natural "Buildings"

On May 31, 1805, before the Corps of Discovery reached the Great Falls, the travelers passed through the White Cliffs region of the Missouri Breaks. The Breaks are the name for the rocky ledges, steep cliffs, and grassy plains surrounding the river. The sandstone formations called the White Cliffs resembled an ancient city. Lewis wrote that the cliffs "with the help of a little immagination [imagination] . . . are made to represent eligant [elegant] ranges of lofty freestone buildings."

The easternmost waterfalls of the Missouri River that the expedition encountered, Great Falls, is the site of a **hydroelectric** dam in today's Montana.

CROSSING THE CONTINENTAL DIVIDE

On August 9, 1805, Lewis and three others left the main group to find the Shoshones. They followed a Native American path through the Rocky Mountains, leaving Montana and entering Idaho. They crossed the Continental Divide on August 12.

Lewis climbed a ridge and looked west. He saw "*ranges of high mountains still to the West of us with their tops partially covered with snow.*" The expedition couldn't continue without horses.

On August 17, the expedition reunited at a Shoshone village. To everyone's surprise, the chief was Sacagawea's brother, Cameahwait. The expedition learned about the land ahead from the Shoshones and prepared for the next stage of the journey. At the end of August, they set out with horses and a Shoshone guide named Old Toby.

LOOKING BACK

Clark described his impression of the Shoshone leader Cameahwait: "The Great Chief . . . is a man of Influence Sence [sense] & easey [easy] & reserved manners, appears to possess a great deel [deal] of Cincerity [sincerity]."

What Is the Continental Divide?

The Continental Divide, sometimes called the Great Divide, is a north-south line of mountain peaks in western North America. It is the dividing line separating waters flowing west and those flowing east. Most of the divide runs along the summits of the Rocky Mountains, through British Columbia and along the British Columbia–Alberta border in Canada, and through Montana, Wyoming, Colorado, and New Mexico. It stretches south into Mexico and Central America.

This 1918 painting shows the expedition being welcomed by the Shoshones. Notice Sacagawea embracing a loved one on the right. The place where the Corps of Discovery met up with the Shoshones was named Camp Fortunate.

THE BITTER BITTERROOTS

On September 11, 1805, the Corps of Discovery began to cross the range of the Rockies called the Bitterroot Mountains. Weather was cold and wet, and the mountains were steep. Fallen trees made climbing difficult. After three days, Clark wrote, "9 miles over a high mountain steep & almost inaxcessible [inaccessible] much falling timber which fatigues our men & horses exceedingly, in stepping over so great a number of logs added to the steep assents [ascents] and decents [descents] of the mountains . . . rained and snowed & hailed the greater part of the day all wet and cold."

Sick, cold, and short of food, they killed and ate some of their horses. At the end of September, the starving explorers made it out of the mountains and found themselves among the Nez Percé people.

LOOKING BACK

The Nez Percé call themselves the Nimiipuu, which means "The People." French Canadian fur traders called them Nez Percé (Pierced Nose) in the 1700s, although the people didn't pierce their noses.

No Harm

According to Nez Percé stories that have been passed down, some wanted to kill the expedition at first. However, an elderly woman named Watkuweis prevented it, saying, "Do them no harm." The legend says she had once been kidnapped by another tribe and taken to Canada. Finally, Europeans helped her escape and find her way back. She returned the kindness by keeping the Nez Percé from killing the explorers.

Nez Percé warrior, 1832

The expedition worried about starving to death in the Bitterroot Mountains. Clark named a stream they discovered in them "Hungry Creek."

SICKNESS STRIKES

The journey through the Bitterroot Mountains had taken its toll on the expedition. They had to stop and rest with the Nez Percé. Clark wrote, "Capt. Lewis & 2 men Verry Sick this evening, my hip Verry Painfull." He recorded similar trouble the next day: "Capt. Lewis scercely [scarcely] able to ride on a jentle horse which was furnished by the Chief, Several men So unwell that they were Compelled to lie on the Side of the road for Some time."

When some expedition members were well enough, they began to build canoes. The rest of the journey would be by river. Finally, on October 7, the expedition put five new canoes into the Clearwater River near present-day Orofino, Idaho, and headed west.

LOOKING BACK

William Clark said he and "th[e] Chief [Twisted Hair, or Walamottinin] & 2 young men went down to hunt timber for Canoes." The Native Americans showed the expedition how fire could be used to hollow out pine trees to shape canoes.

Stomach Troubles

Although the expedition brought food with them–including 93 pounds (42 kg) of dried soup!–they went through it quickly. Sometimes their diet caused digestive troubles. Clark recorded in September 1805: "We have nothing to eate [eat] but roots, which give the men violent pains in their bowels after eating much of them . . . I am verry sick all night, Pane [pain] in Stomach & the bowels oweing [owing] to my diet."

This sculpture in Boise, Idaho, shows Meriwether Lewis in a three-cornered hat and William Clark wearing a fur cap. Nez Percé tribal leader Twisted Hair motions to the west, while his son looks at traded goods on the ground.

ALMOST THERE

The Clearwater River's current helped the expedition make quick progress. But they found the Snake River hard to travel because of its many **rapids**, and the Columbia River too had falls and rapids. Clark said they "should make more portages [but] time [is] precious with us." Supplies were lost when canoes overturned or sank.

Excitement rippled through the expedition on November 7, 1805. They thought they saw and heard the Pacific Ocean. Clark wrote, "Great joy in camp we are in viuew [view] of the Ocian [ocean], this great Pacific Octean [Ocean] which we been so long anxious to See." They were wrong, though. What they saw was a bay. The Pacific was still 20 miles (32 km) away. Bad weather kept them from reaching the coast for another three weeks.

LOOKING BACK

The hard November rains kept the Corps of Discovery from traveling to the coast. Clark wrote, "We are all wet and disagreeable" many times in his journal.

Final Obstacles

As the expedition approached the Pacific, they encountered the Chinook people. The Chinook had been trading with Europeans for years. In fact, Clark complained about the Native Americans' prices for the things they needed, but the Chinook said the Europeans paid them well. Lewis traded for a Chinook canoe, which was wide, light, and easy to **maneuver**. The expedition also hired Chinook river guides since the fog was too thick at times to see where they were going.

The expedition was able to obtain food from Native Americans along the way. Clark noted that Sacagawea "**reconciles** all the Indians, as to our friendly intentions."

WINTER ON THE PACIFIC COAST

In mid-November 1805, over a year after the expedition began, the Corps of Discovery reached the Pacific Coast. Clark reported the expedition's members were "much Satisfied with their trip beholding with estonishment [astonishment] the high waves dashing against the rocks & this emence [immense] ocean." They chose a spot near the present-day city of Astoria, Oregon, to build their winter fort. They named it Fort Clatsop after nearby Native Americans.

Even though they had reached their destination, the expedition's journal entries reflect misery caused by the weather. Clark complained about rain, wind, and hail. But on December 30, the day they finished the fort, he said: "This day proved to be the fairest and best which we have had since our arrival at thjis [this] place, only three Showers dureing [during] this whole day."

LOOKING BACK

On the coast, William Clark estimated the expedition had traveled 4,162 miles (6,698 km). This was within 40 miles (64 km) of the actual distance.

The Whale

Around the time the expedition was finishing Fort Clatsop at the end of December, Native Americans told them a whale had washed up on the beach. Days later, Clark took a small group to find out if they could trade for whale **blubber** to add to their diet. Clark said the whale's "Skeleton measured 105 feet" (32 m). The expedition also traded for whale oil, which they probably used for food and as a fuel for oil lamps.

Before returning east, the expedition gave Fort Clatsop to the neighboring Clatsop people.

THE JOURNEY HOME

After a cold, wet winter, the expedition was ready to return home. Lewis and Clark had hoped to see ships on the Pacific that could take them back east. They found none, though, and headed inland in late March 1806.

The explorers reached the Nez Percé in early May 1806 and retrieved their horses from them. However, they had to wait weeks for the snow to melt enough to cross the Bitterroots. In early July, they split into groups to explore more of the Louisiana Territory.

In mid-August, the groups rejoined where the Yellowstone and Missouri Rivers met. They entered St. Louis, Missouri, on September 23, 1806. Clark reported, "We were met by all the village." Celebrations were held in their honor. The incredible journey of the Lewis and Clark Expedition was complete.

LOOKING BACK

Lewis's return party killed two Blackfeet Indians after a fight broke out in July 1806.

Sacagawea's Legacy

The explorers returned Sacagawea, Toussaint Charbonneau, and their baby Jean Baptiste (nicknamed Pompey) to the Mandan villages before traveling on. It isn't certain what happened to Sacagawea after that. Some say she died in 1812, after giving birth to a daughter. Others think she rejoined the Shoshones and died much later, in 1884. She is still honored today for her role in the expedition, including with a U.S. dollar coin.

Lewis and Clark Expedition Map

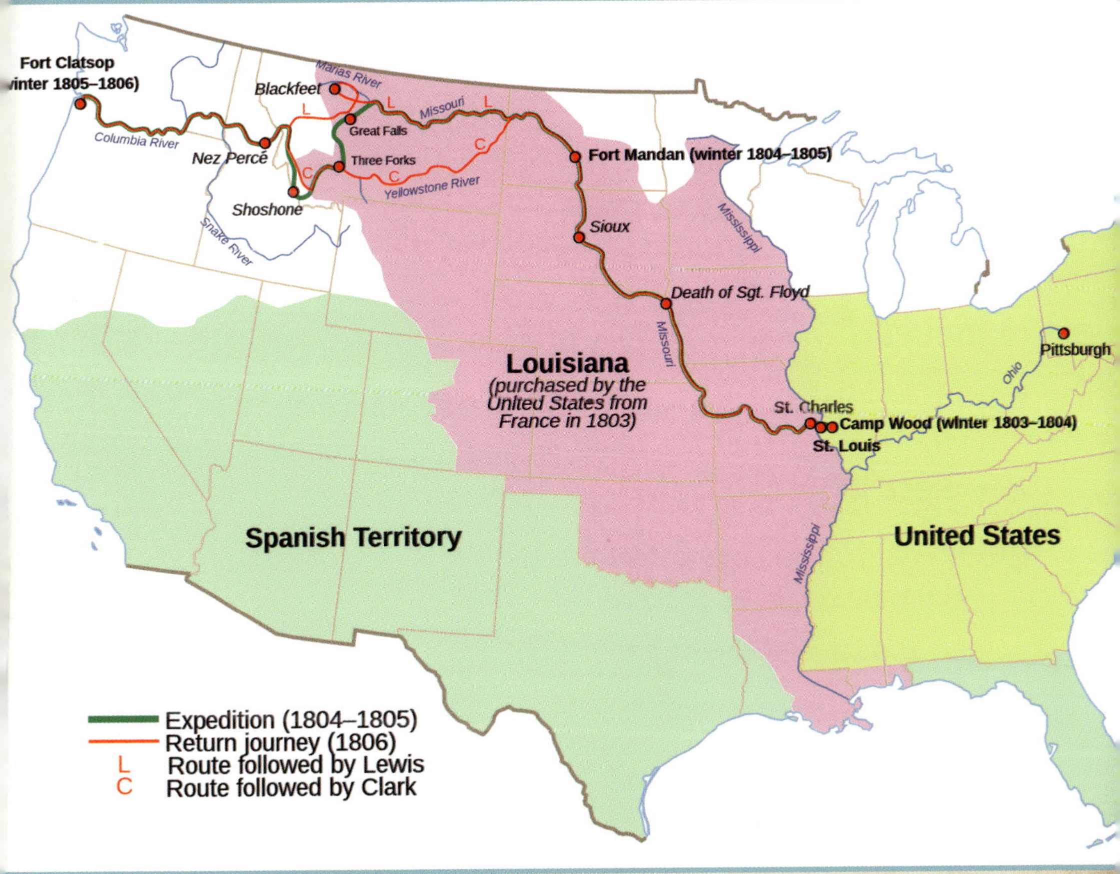

The expedition didn't find a water route to the Pacific Ocean. However, their maps were invaluable, and they opened trade with many Native American peoples.

GLOSSARY

blubber: The fat of a whale or other ocean creature.

corps: A group of people working together with a common purpose.

cultural: Having to do with the beliefs and ways of life of a group of people.

frenzy: Intense or wild activity.

frostbite: A medical condition in which parts of the body freeze or almost freeze.

hydroelectric: Relating to or used in the production of electricity by waterpower.

malady: Illness.

maneuver: To move skillfully around.

punctuation: The marks, including periods (.) and commas (,), that are used to make the meaning of a piece of writing clear.

quill: A stiff, sharp, pointed hair on the body of some animals.

rapid: A part of a river with a swift current and obstacles such as large rocks.

reconcile: To cause people to become friendly or in agreement.

tepee: A home shaped like a cone used in the past by some Native Americans.

FOR MORE INFORMATION

Books

Davis, Hasan. *The Journey of York: The Unsung Hero of the Lewis and Clark Expedition*. North Mankato, MN: Capstone Editions, 2019.

Keppeler, Jill. *Team Time Machine Tags Along with Lewis and Clark*. New York, NY: Gareth Stevens Publishing, 2021.

Shea, Therese. *The Louisiana Purchase and the Lewis and Clark Expedition*. New York, NY: Britannica Educational Publishing, 2018.

Websites

Journals of the Lewis & Clark Expedition
lewisandclarkjournals.unl.edu/
Read the journals of expedition members and see sketches they made.

Lewis and Clark National Historic Trail
www.nps.gov/lecl/index.htm
Today's adventurers can follow in the Corps of Discovery's footsteps.

Publisher's note to educators and parents: Our editors have carefully reviewed these websites to ensure that they are suitable for students. Many websites change frequently, however, and we cannot guarantee that a site's future contents will continue to meet our high standards of quality and educational value. Be advised that students should be closely supervised whenever they access the internet.

INDEX